Other books by A. K. Yearling

Daring Do and the Quest for the Sapphire Stone

Daring Do and the Griffon's Goblet

Daring Do and the Abyss of Despair

Daring Do and the Razor of Dreams

Daring Do and the Ring of Destiny

Daring Do and the Trek to the Terrifying Tower

Daring Do and the Volcano of Destiny

Daring Do and the Marked Thief of Marapore

Daring Do and the Eternal Flower

Daring Do and the Forbidden City of Clouds

Other books by G. M. Berrow

Twilight Sparkle and the Crystal Heart Spell

Pinkie Pie and the Rockin' Ponypalooza Party!

Rainbow Dash and the Daring Do Double Dare

Rarity and the Curious Case of Charity

Applejack and the Honest-to-Goodness Switcheroo

By A. K. Yearling
with G. M. Berrow

Little, Brown and Company
New York Boston

Little, Brown and Company

Hachette Book Group
1290 Avenue of the Americas, New York, NY 10104
Visit us at lb-kids.com

Little, Brown and Company is a division of Hachette Book Group, Inc.
The Little, Brown name and logo are trademarks of
Hachette Book Group, Inc.

The publisher is not responsible for websites (or their content)
that are not owned by the publisher.

First Stand-Alone Edition: July 2016
Originally published as part of *My Little Pony: The Daring Do Adventure
Collection* in October 2014 by Little, Brown and Company

Library of Congress Control Number: 2014940996

ISBN 978-0-316-38938-9

10 9 8 7 6 5 4 3 2 1

RRD-C

Printed in the United States of America

To Lauren—who kept her head
in the clouds so our imaginations
could take flight

TABLE OF CONTENTS

CHAPTER 1

The Deserted Trail Past Copper Bit Canyon

"There she is!" the ponies shouted. "Seize her! Giddyup!" The voices woke Daring Do from a sleep so deep that she had almost forgotten where she was. A quick glance around reminded the pony adventurer that she was still in a tent in the middle of nowhere, with nopony but herself to rely on.

After five days spent crossing the San Palomino Desert and battling the dry, energy-sapping heat and the raging sandstorms, Daring Do was now going to have to protect the jewel-encrusted Doomed Diadem of Xilati from some ruffian cowponies who didn't know what was good for them. *Again*.

The yellow Pegasus adjusted her tan pith helmet with the green band around it and peered through a rip in the side of her crude hut. Through the swathe of dusty canvas, Daring Do could see the shadowed outlines of the gang on the horizon. She sighed heavily, like a pony who has to keep swatting mosquitoes away.

Ever since Daring retrieved the Diadem from its crumbling shrine on the edge of the desert, there had been several gangs of thieves hot on her gray-and-black tail. She thought she'd lost all of them for good, having been alone for almost a whole day. She'd reckoned that a few hours spent shaded from the harsh rays were harmless enough.

Daring silently cursed herself for falling asleep, but it was too late for regrets. There was only time to take action and defend her treasure. Luckily, Daring Do was the one pony who was practically made for the task.

"Give us the crown, Darin' Do!" a brown stallion shouted. He was no longer shrouded in silhouette. She noted his familiar wide-brimmed cowpony hat and dusty red kerchief.

When her quest had taken her across the San Palomino, Daring Do had suspected that the Wild Bunch Gang might turn up. Slingshot and his ragtag robber sidekicks, North Star and Spaghetti Slim, would stop at nothing to bag some loot. But these fortune seekers were different from her—their research and their motives were sloppy. All they cared about was money. It didn't matter to them whether it was stolen bits from a bank or a priceless relic rescued from a crumbling temple. If the item in question would buy them cider and other favors from their boss, Old Tex, it was theirs for the taking. Except if it belonged to Daring Do, of course. Apparently, this was a lesson she was going to have to teach them again.

"Nice try, Slingshot!" Daring Do burst forth from the hut, scooping up the sparkling Diadem and other belongings in one swift motion. She whipped her foreleg around, snagged the fabric of her tent, and let the canvas wrap everything into a neat package. She then swung the strap across her shoulder and smoothed down the collar of her green adventure shirt, checking to make sure her map was still in the left chest pocket.

Daring Do puffed up and shouted across the expanse, "You're wasting your energy, cowponies! Take my advice and save some of that giddyup to get back to your camp before Old Tex catches you and turns your hide into his new holsters! You're *never* getting the crown from me!"

"Is that so?!" Slingshot called back, kicking his forelegs up to challenge her.

"Unfortunately for you...*yes*." Out of the corner of her eye, Daring Do scanned the surroundings but felt like she was looking through a fish-eye lens. The haze of sleep hadn't completely worn off, and she'd been traveling for days.

There was a distinctive cactus in the distance that Daring remembered seeing the last time she trekked through this way. It looked like a big, prickly hot air balloon. She recalled that it was near the border of the desert, but also recalled that it was at least another four hours' walk before there were any pony towns to disappear into.

The open desert left her nowhere to lie low. The only cover was a smattering of spiky green cacti plants in sparse clumps and gigantic tumbleweeds blowing across the ground every so often. The only way to lose the Wild Bunch Gang this time would be by flying up into the cloudless sky. But North Star, Slingshot's right-hoof pony, was a Pegasus, too. And though the burly navy-blue stallion was a little slow on the uptake, he was pretty fast in the air. A sky chase could go on just as long as a land one.

Daring kept a stony expression. Maybe she could win this one by coercion. "I'd advise you all"—she raised an eyebrow and motioned with her hoof—"to move along, lil' ponies."

"I'm afraid we can't do that, ma'am." Slingshot smirked through the scruff on his face. "See...we've been followin' ya ever since ya passed through Copper Bit Canyon." Slingshot narrowed his blue eyes and took off his hat—revealing a flat blue mane that clung to his head with sweat. He pretended to be very concentrated on rubbing some dirt off the brim of his hat as he spoke—a tactic to show how disinterested he was in anything Daring had to say or do, when really it was just the opposite. "That trek through Rattlesnake Gulch was no trot in the park on a Sunday, either."

"Really?" Daring Do laughed, taking a few steps closer. "I had no problem with those snakes! You and your boys sure are getting soft...."

"Look here, lil' lady!" North Star coughed as he wiped his brow with his white kerchief. He looked like he was about to go hooves up from the stifling dry heat. Maybe he wouldn't be able to outfly her after all. "You expectin' us to leave the treasure when we…uh…need it?! I mean, *we* should get it 'cause you have it, and we're wantin' it and, uh…" He looked down at his hooves in confusion.

Slingshot rolled his eyes. "I think what my buddy here is *trying* to say is that we *ain't* goin' back empty-hoofed!"

"Yeah!" North Star nodded. "Full-hoofed!"

Spaghetti swung his rope lasso, hoping to drum up some fear. "So just toss over the crown, and nopony needs to get hurt!"

"You're done, Do!" Slingshot nodded

in agreement. "That crown is ours as sure as a tumbleweed tumbles!"

"That's your problem right there, fellas." Daring chuckled. She patted the treasure, safely tucked into her makeshift canvas bag. "You don't even know *what* it is you're trying to steal from me." Daring Do reached inside and pulled the Diadem out into plain sight. The stallions gasped. "Just because I'm such a history buff, you'll have to indulge me…."

"Hoof it here!" Slingshot growled, stomping the ground with his hooves.

"How about a lesson?" Daring continued, ignoring the command. "This beauty here is the Doomed Diadem of Xilati, and it belonged to the Empress of the Desert Skies…." Daring Do smoothed a hoof over the golden relic, which was encrusted with stunning sapphires and diamonds. Rays of desert sun bore down on the treasure, causing hundreds of tiny rainbows to reflect and shine onto the dirty, grumpy gang of robbers. They were trying to act tough and menacing but had sparkles all over them! Daring Do found the disparity of the sight amusing.

"The ancient texts say that this crown belongs with its sister—the Tiara of Teotlale, which was worn by the Empress of the Desert Sands. Legend says Teotlale loved her sister Xilati so much that she wished they could be together, always. When Xilati was married off to another empire, Teotlale missed her so much that she cursed the jewels forever!" She dangled the crown in front of Slingshot. He couldn't tear his greedy eyes away, and reached his hoof toward it....

"That's why it's 'doomed,' get it?" Daring Do winked and yanked the crown back, trotting back to her spot. "Because if one of the two crowns is without the other for more than fourteen moons, the night will become *eternal*...for everypony!" Daring lowered her voice to a whisper. "It's a good thing I know where the Tiara of Teotlale is being kept, since it was stolen thirteen moons ago...."

"What a load of rotten hay!" North Star grumbled, and spit a large wad of apple chewing taffy on the ground. He leaned forward and spread his wings out, preparing to take off. "I'm real tired of talkin',

Sling. Next thing ya know, she's gonna be sayin' that the Halo in the Sky is real, too. And everypony knows it ain't—"

"Hush yer muzzle!" Slingshot held up a hoof to silence his comrade. "I got this!"

"Do you?!" Daring Do shouted over her shoulder as she broke into a gallop, heading away from the gang. Clouds of beige dust billowed up, creating a sandy haze. When it cleared, the ponies saw a train chugging along in the distance, heading straight toward them.

CHAPTER 2
Losing the Wild Bunch Gang

Daring Do glanced back at the massive locomotive careening in their direction but kept up her pace, running alongside the tracks. Slingshot and his boys chased after her, calling out gibberish commands to one another over the noise. It sounded like they were going to try to corral her like a cow. Daring laughed to herself at the notion.

The adventurer slowed down slightly, letting the boys gain on her. Then, right as Spaghetti tossed his lasso at her, Daring Do spread her wings and soared to the top of one of the train cars. North Star and Spaghetti ran straight into each other, tumbling to the dusty ground in a heap. But Slingshot didn't miss a beat. He hoisted himself into an open door of one of the cars, which was filled with bales of hay and fat, oinking pigs. "Get offa me, swine!" he cursed at a snarfing piggy who began to lick him as if he were a snack.

Up above, Daring Do ran along the top of the moving train, wings outspread. She was about to spring up into the sky when she saw an opening in the caboose. *Perfect*. If she could hop in and close the trapdoor, she would be able to shut Slingshot out! The Pegasus looked back over her shoulder. Her pursuer was covered in pig muck and struggling to find his hoofing on the roof. The mud was making it difficult for him to get a firm grip. "I'm gonna getcha!" he shouted with a wild spark in his eye.

The puffs of smoke coming from the chimney wafted back into his face, causing him to sputter and cough. Daring used the opportunity to lower herself into the open door, leaving it slightly propped open, and then hang on to the lip of the opening. She looked down and saw two snarling tigers—not a place she could stay for long. A few seconds later, Slingshot's face appeared right above her, blocking the whole passage. If he slammed the door shut, Daring Do would be stuck in the train car with no way out.

"You're trapped now, Daring Do!" Slingshot smiled in wicked triumph, his mane blowing in the rushing wind as the desert scenery whipped past them. "Give me the crown or you're riding all the way to the Frozen North with your new friends!" The tigers growled in response, circling below as the two ponies negotiated.

"It's a *Diadem*." Daring snarled, pulling her body up so her face was right next to his. "And it belongs with its sister...in a *museum*!" Daring then grabbed Slingshot's lasso, wrapped it around him, and then swung his whole body over to the next car. He fell right into another open trapdoor, screaming.

Daring flew up out of the car, and over to the open door. She shouted down at Slingshot, who had landed in a big pile of elephant dung. "Maybe you can visit the exhibition sometime, Slingshot. Tell 'em Daring Do sent you!"

Slingshot grunted in response, trying to rub the dung from his eyes. Daring waited so he could watch her fly off into the sky, victorious.

CHAPTER 3
Rescuing Ravenhoof

Daring Do knocked the heavy brass horse-shoe on the antique wooden door again. "Hellooooo? Anypony home?" She cocked her head to the side and listened carefully. Voices. Two of them. She waited another second before calling out, "Ravenhoof, you old chump, open the door! I need a shower and something to eat! Oh, and I've got a theory that you'll be interested in about the special treat I've brought you. It's the Dia—" The door swung open, and A. B. Ravenhoof appeared, looking frazzled. His fuzzy green cardigan was buttoned incorrectly, and his wire-framed glasses sat crooked on the bridge of his face. Daring Do smiled. "You look terrible."

"Shhhhhh!" Ravenhoof hissed, holding a hoof to Daring's muzzle. "Not another peep." He backed into the house slowly, motioning to the closet in the corner. "Ah, so good to see you again, *Compass Rose*! But I'm actually in the middle of something right now...."

"So sorry to barge in, sir," Daring Do replied, picking up on the hint that she was playing the part of somepony named Compass Rose. There was clearly some sort of hostage situation or raid in progress. "I'll just need a moment of your time. Surely you can spare that?"

Ravenhoof smiled nervously. "Of course. How about some sweet dandelion tea? That's your favorite, isn't it?"

"So good of you to remember!" Daring Do answered in a voice that sounded like it might belong to a fancier pony than she. "Two sugar lumps and an apple biscuit as well, if you have any." She sank down into a flowered armchair and pretended to read from the book on the side table while Ravenhoof puttered about in the kitchen. She surveyed the quiet room. Everything *looked* to be in order, but she could feel that there was definitely something off. "Achoo!" A muffled sneeze came from the direction of the closet. Aha! So the mystery pony was hiding in there. *How inconvenient.* All Daring wanted right now was to show her hard-won prize to Ravenhoof and get the Diadem of Xilati back to the Tiara of Teotlale. They were running out of time.

It seemed that the only way to do that was to get rid of this other minor obstacle first. Without another thought, Daring Do sprang forward across the room, hind leg extended out in front of her body. Her hoof smashed against the closet door, busting it wide open to reveal a crouched figure struggling to hide beneath a mountain of cloaks and hats. "I see you," Daring Do declared. "Whoever you are... come out before I— Eeeugh!" Daring suddenly felt her body spin and slam to the ground. She twisted back around and saw that the offender was a pale gray pony with a purple shirt collar around his neck and a cutie mark of a purple-and-yellow explosion surrounded by four black stars. His short black mane was rumpled, and he was grinning wickedly. She knew this stallion—it was Withers, one of Dr. Caballeron's henchponies! He normally wore dark sunglasses, but he must have lost them in the closet.

Daring Do flung the Diadem to Ravenhoof's desk and rolled across the floor, away from Withers. She wasn't sure what he was after, but if Withers could get his hooves on the treasure, he surely would try to steal away with it—just like everything else Daring Do discovered.

"Withers!" Daring Do shouted as she sprang back to her hooves. "What are *you* doing here?" She took a step closer, leaning in, a look of suspicion on her face. "Is Caballeron ahoof, too?"

The pony laughed haughtily and jumped onto the wooden dining table, his eyes darting up to the ceiling every few seconds. He began to jump toward the rusty ceiling lamp. There was something hidden up there, and he wanted it very badly. Ravenhoof's place was full of items of extreme worth, so there was no telling what it might be. She still had to protect it.

"Hey!" Daring growled as she spread her wings and flew across the room. She hovered right above Withers's head and tried to meet his gaze, but he continued to ignore her and just kept reaching for the lamp. Once he finally grabbed the shade, he began to swing back and forth, using the cord of the lamp much like Daring Do used vines in the jungle to get around. His technique was sloppy. Clearly, Withers wasn't the most athletic pony. It was becoming obvious to Daring Do that this was a solo mission. Without backup, he didn't stand a chance.

"I. Asked. You. A. Question!" Daring bellowed, growing impatient. "Where is Caballeron?" She began to whizz around him, hoping to fluster and confuse him. Withers soon lost his grip and came crashing down to the ground, taking the lamp along, too. His eyes shot back up to the spot he had been trying to reach, and Daring Do finally saw the object of his desire— a rolled-up piece of parchment on the highest bookshelf. Was all this fuss over a little scroll? There could be anything written on it. It must be juicy. Now Daring Do felt an intense desire to have it, too.

"I know what you're after, Withers," Daring bluffed, pinning Withers to the ground. "And there's no way you're getting it. Go now and I might spare telling Caballeron how you were too much of a coward to even talk to me. This can stay between us."

Withers grunted in defeat, nodded, and pulled himself up. The pony darted to the corner, scooped up his sunglasses from the ground, and put them back on his face. He took off out the door without so much as a glance back at the house.

Daring Do chuckled to herself as she

watched him gallop away. What a feeble attempt at thievery that had been.

"All right, here we *are!*" Ravenhoof entered the room again, holding a tray with a kitschy tea set. Steam rose from the spout of the pot in inviting swirls. He was speaking in a very loud stage voice, emphasizing random words here and there for the benefit of the intruder. "I think I *managed* to rustle up some *tasty,* er...tidbits!" Then he noticed the gigantic mess of furniture turned over and the lamp torn from the ceiling. Ravenhoof's jaw dropped. "What in the blazes did you do, Do?!" His eyes darted to the closet.

"Oh, he's gone." Daring rubbed her hooves together as if wiping them clean from the job. She looked back over her shoulder with a smirk. "Took care of your business...so we could get to mine."

The old pony did another double take toward the closet, which was wide open, an avalanche of outerwear tumbling out onto the floor. Part of him looked utterly befuddled at how so much could have happened in such a short amount of time. But as an ex-adventurer and instigator himself, he didn't seem all that surprised. "Well, that's solved, then."

"Now, what was I saying?" Daring Do reached into her saddlebag and procured the glittering crown. "Oh *right*. Priceless relic that I rescued from several gangs of San Palomino robbers just in time to reunite it with its sister so we're not all doomed to darkness forever?" She twirled the crown around a little so it could catch the light and look even more impressive.

"Great Trot!!" Ravenhoof dropped the tray with the tea and biscuits. Everything clattered to the ground and slid across the floor. He rushed forward with a look of reverence on his face and gingerly took the crown from Daring's hooves. "You actually did it," Ravenhoof marveled, turning the Diadem over to inspect every jewel, inscription, and crevice. "You located the Diadem of Xilati in time!"

"Actually, if we're counting, it's a day early." Daring Do tipped her helmet. "But who's counting?" she joked. It was a favorite game of theirs—challenging each other to quests and seeing how fast they could be completed. Sometimes they bet some bits, other times it was just for fun. These days, with Ravenhoof's advancing age, it was more often him giving the challenges and Daring going on the adventures.

"I guess I owe you some bits, you smug mare." Ravenhoof smiled and trotted over to his desk. He reached for a magnifying glass. "I thought for sure that the Diadem was lost forever after the Tiara of Teotlale turned up in that gypsy marketplace by the river. I thought we were going to experience firsthoof whether or not the legend of the curse was true." Ravenhoof motioned to a shelf in the corner, stacked high with waxy white cylinders. "I've even been stocking up on candles!"

"What for?" Daring Do shook her head at the old pony. "A vigil for my lost pride?"

"Eternal night and all that." He shrugged,

bringing his attention back to more important matters. "But we don't have to worry about that now." He held the crown up to the magnifying glass, which he had pressed up against his right eye. "Fascinating! See that ridge right there?" He ran his hoof along a jagged section on the Diadem, which looked a little bit like the skyline of an Equestrian city. "It's the exact opposite of the one on the Sand Empress's tiara! I think the two crowns can lock together!" His green eyes were alight with intrigue—it looked like he'd all but forgotten that he had just been held hostage a few moments earlier. A. B. Ravenhoof moved on quickly. "Let's see, shall we?"

Ravenhoof trotted to the lowest level of his bookshelf, ran his hoof along the dusty titles, and then pulled a particularly thick spine out. It was dark blue with bronzed letters that read *Fungi of the Southern Forests*. Suddenly, a little door on the back wall of the bookcase swung open. Inside was a metal safe, locked with a gigantic rusty padlock! Ravenhoof fumbled with a ring of keys on his belt and located the lock's partner, muttering something to himself all the while. Daring Do craned to see the other contents of the safe, but the old adventurer found what he was looking for pretty fast—a small blue box. Then he slammed it shut, before turning his attention back to the two crowns.

"Hey, Professor?"

"Yes, Daring?" Ravenhoof replied without tearing his eyes away from the task of trying to fit the two crowns together. It wasn't working.

"What do you suppose that pony

wanted?" Daring sat down on a plaid sofa. "Caballeron's fellow? Withers is his name. Unless you've been held hostage in your own home more than once today?" Daring Do joked.

"No, just the once. I wasn't really being held, you know," said Ravenhoof. "It was just for sport. I was bored and thought it might be fun to keep him around for a while as company."

"Of course!" The story seemed unlikely, but Daring Do went along with it anyway. She raised an eyebrow. "Well, just so you know, he seemed pretty keen on stealing something from up there." Daring pointed to the rolled-up parchment on the highest shelf. "What's on that scroll?"

"Oh, that's just my recipe for banana flaxseed muffins." Ravenhoof laughed. "I must have kept looking up there while he was questioning me. There's a spider in that corner that I've been meaning to get rid of for a while." He adjusted his glasses and looked back to the crowns again. "Anyway, he seemed to think I had information on Cirrostrata. He kept asking me for a map...."

"Cirrostrata?" Daring repeated, scanning the corners of her mind for the name. It didn't even sound familiar. "What's that?"

"The Forbidden City of Clouds! The invisible city of the sky!" The professor put the crowns down on the desk and trotted over to join Daring Do. "Don't tell me you've never heard of it!"

Daring shook her head. She never liked to admit to not having the answers, but her interest was piqued. The word *forbidden* in particular always made her want to do the exact opposite of what it advised.

"It's very dangerous...." Ravenhoof looked up from his task, a grave expression on his face. "Cirrostrata is rumored to be a place unlike any other in this world. A city of cloud dwellers that are said to be so secretive that any outsider who has attempted to enter its walls has never returned." Ravenhoof stood up, looking her straight in the eye. "That's why so little is known about it. Also, it's invisible."

"Then how is it possible that we know it exists at all?" Daring Do questioned. "It could just be a fantasy—some sort of fairy tale." There had been enough false leads in her career for Daring Do not to trust everything she heard. Ravenhoof, however, was one of her most reliable sources.

He knew what made her tick, because he ticked the same way.

The old professor let out a heavy sigh. "Well, there is one pony who claims to have been there. His name's Brumby. Brumby Cloverpatch. But—"

"But what?" Daring Do interrupted. The excitement was growing in the pit of her stomach. "I must find him!"

"I doubt he would be willing to help. The whole ordeal ruined his career. Used to be one of the most famous explorers in the world. But after he discovered Cirrostrata and failed to recover the treasure—the Halo—he never adventured again. Nopony knows what happened to him up there." Ravenhoof shook his head in despair, a deep triangle of crinkles forming on his brow. "Bit of a pity, really. And such a mystery!" He searched Daring's face and realized that there was no stopping her.

"If anypony can get him to talk, it's me." Daring Do stood up, wearing a proud smirk on her face. "I'm going to find him. Then I'm going to get to Cirrostrata and I'm going to retrieve that treasure. Mark my words."

The Diadem and the Tiara in his hooves finally fit together with a resounding click. "I don't doubt it." A. B. Ravenhoof shook his head and laughed. "But at least have some tea first."

CHAPTER 4
Reſt and Realization

After a few hours' rest on the squashy sofa, a hot Epsom salt–lick bath, and a hearty meal of carroty potato mash, Daring Do was feeling much better. The pony adventurer was more than ready to get started on her search for Brumby Cloverpatch and the mysterious cloud city he had discovered long ago. Just the notion of the treasured "Halo of Cirrostrata" had the young pony making all sorts of speculations about what exactly the item could be, and whether or not it was all that the ponies up there were hiding. It was always possible that this guy Brumby had made the entire thing up. But something deep inside her gut told her she could trust the facts.

Either way, Brumby's story was intriguing, and Daring Do longed to know more. She just hoped she'd be able to find him and pry some answers out. From the little information she had to go on—a few letters to Ravenhoof and an old photograph—it might be difficult to recognize him. Especially since he didn't want to be found anymore.

Daring had fallen asleep studying the photo, and now it was permanently committed to her memory. The shot was faded and only in black and white, but just from this one look, she could tell Brumby was cut from the same unique cloth as she. A true adventurer with the world as his oyster.

The burly stallion had a frizzy mane, long sideburns, and a twinkle in his eyes. He had an interesting style of clothing. Brumby sported a shiny top hat and a striped waistcoat, almost as if he were a time traveler visiting from the early days of Equestria. On his lapel sat a shiny pin in the shape of a crest. It was hard to make out, but the etching on it looked like a hot air balloon. When Daring Do had pointed it out to Ravenhoof, he'd put on his glasses and brought it close to his face. "Aeronauts Society," he'd proclaimed with a nod. "Cloverpatch must have bought it at an antiques market. He always was a big fan of the history of Earth-pony flight."

Daring Do wasn't sure what to do with the information, but it seemed important, so she scribbled down the details in her notebook for later. Then she got back to work on packing her things. She hated to idle for too long and would hopefully be on her way toward Cirrostrata that very night.

"Do you think that'll tide you over?" A. B. Ravenhoof pointed to the provisions on the desk. He bit his lip in concern and took a sip of tea. In addition to the information he had on Brumby, he'd managed to rustle up a pair of high-altitude weatherproof goggles, some chewing gum, a store of crusty bread, and all the apple biscuits that were left in the cupboard. It was too bad he'd lost his detailed map of the Unicorn Mountain Range. Come to think of it, he hadn't seen it in years.

"This is more than enough to get me to the mountains and to the town of Alto Terre." Daring Do nodded, surveying the stores. "It should only be a three-day journey if I fly the whole way."

"Surely you aren't planning that, with your bad wing and all...."

Daring could see the unease in the old pony's eyes. He was becoming soft in his old age. She put a hoof on the professor's shoulder. "Don't worry about me, Rave. I'll be *fine!*" Daring was always more concerned about finding the object of her desire than bothering with silly logistics. Things like food and water always had a way of working themselves out. "You really think Cloverpatch is still living there?"

"Well, it's the last place he was seen," said Ravenhoof, pulling out his hanky and starting to wring it nervously. "But… as with *all* adventurers, you never can be sure they'll stay in one spot for too long. In fact, I think I am going to abandon this place today! How about you come with me to Horseshoe Bay instead? I think I have a new lead on the Crystal Sphere of Khumn…."

"That *is* tempting, but Cirrostrata can't

wait!" Daring Do looked out the window to the sky. She felt the excitement rising in her chest.

"If you insist." Ravenhoof sighed. Sure, it was true that he had seen just as many horrors throughout his adventures as she had, but sometimes he felt protective of her. Throughout her career, Daring Do had often come to him seeking his advice, even though she was anything but fragile.

In the time Ravenhoof had known her, Daring had come such a long way. He was very proud of her, almost like she was a daughter. He recalled the time a few years before when Daring had trouble overcoming her deep, dark secret fear of fish. The churning, piranha-filled moat surrounding the Dark Tower was proving to be a major hindrance in her quest to reach the Radiant Shield of Razdon, which was hidden deep inside its corridors. At the time, Daring Do was desperate—she didn't know if she could even fly over the waters without completely freezing up and falling in. She'd visited Ravenhoof and he'd coached her through it. In the end, she had conquered her fears and retrieved the shield with ease.

"How about I come with you?" Ravenhoof joked. They both knew he didn't mean it. The fact that he was an Earth pony would not be helpful in trying to locate a city in the sky, not to mention his advancing age. No—this was a journey that Daring Do must make alone.

"The next time I visit you, I promise it will be for longer," Daring Do assured him, stepping out onto Ravenhoof's porch. "A *real* visit! I am sure I'll have lots of secrets to reveal about Cirrostrata. And a brand-new treasure to deliver, too—the Halo." Daring Do slung her bag over her body, popped on her helmet, and took off into the dusky sky.

CHAPTER 5
Upward and Onward to Alto Terre

As she touched her hooves upon the steep, pine-needle-and-dew-covered ground, Daring Do felt her chest tighten. Since she flew all the time, the Pegasus was no stranger to high altitudes, but the air here in the Unicorn Mountain Range felt especially thin. Instantly, the story sprang to mind of how an ancient Unicorn clan had cast a spell on the area. It was said that the Carthachs loved the beautiful mountains and had done everything in their powers to keep it pure and untouched by other pony hooves. They didn't want to share it with anypony, and to this day, the area was mostly uninhabited.

Or maybe Daring Do was just tired and out of breath and it wasn't the Curse of the Carthachs at all. She searched her bag for a piece of gum and popped it into her mouth. Within a few seconds, her ears depressurized and her breathing returned to normal.

Once she could breathe, the majestic scene around her took hold of her senses. A thick grove of slanted green trees reached up toward the sky. It smelled fresh and piney. The soft terrain below was littered with rocky patches that would serve as excellent hoofholds on her climb. Everything was moist and chilly, like the last snow of the season had finally melted, allowing the emerald hues to take over once more and make way for more moderate temperatures. The last moments before summer.

Looking out to the rest of the Unicorn Range in the distance, Daring Do felt that the mountains seemed at once near and very far away—their colors fading into hazy, pastel versions of the one on which she stood. Daring Do took a long, deep breath. She let her eyes drink in the beauty of the sights and her tired body relax into the atmospheric change. She almost wanted to camp here for a day or two, but there was no time for leisure.

A narrow, winding path in the distance signaled the way to civilization. It was difficult to read the small wooden sign in the shape of an arrow, but she knew what it said. The only town for miles was Alto Terre, a place that was so rarely visited that little could be found about it in her books. As Daring Do began the climb to her fate, she was grateful to feel the solid ground under her hooves and to rest her fatigued wings against her back for a while.

A few hours on the incline and several apple biscuits later, Daring Do had reached the village. The picturesque settlement was just as Brumby had described in his last letter to Ravenhoof, which

Daring Do had burned in her mind after studying it so many times. *Alto Terre is a Unicorn settlement near the peak of Mount Monoceros. It somehow manages to be quaint and tremendous at the same time—a small, bustling city with impressive cottages and a marketplace. The best part is that it's cut off from the rest of the world. Since I am no longer fit to explore, I think I'll stay here in isolation,* he'd written. *It's for the best.*

There were about a hundred multi-storied white cottages with brown roofs precariously built on the sloping mountainside. They faced in every direction, but in some sort of considered pattern, like crooked teeth in a dragon's jaw. Daring Do marveled at the arrangement. It was a wonder that anypony could get up here in the first place, let alone construct such sturdy buildings at such a drastic angle. It must have taken quite a lot of complicated Unicorn magic and many centuries to achieve. Judging by the thick patches of ivy crawling up the sides and the rusted windowpanes on the buildings, this was a very old town.

As she trotted up the last stretch of path before entering Alto Terre, Daring thought of the last few lines of Brumby's letter, and a shiver went up her spine. *Don't try to find me. I wish to be left alone now. To make a new life and forget all that has transpired before. It's the only way.*

It was a mystery whether Brumby Cloverpatch still wished to be left alone, but Daring's guess was that he did. Nopony had heard from him since. Even A. B. Ravenhoof, his old contemporary and friend, had honored his wishes after all these years, claiming that Brumby was not a pony one wanted to cross. If he wanted to be found, he would. This made Daring Do want to talk to him even more. What catastrophic event could have occurred in Cirrostrata to make him give up his love for adventure? Would the same thing happen to her once she found the invisible cloud city? It was all so intriguing.

There was only one way to find out, and it was hiding in one of those buildings.

CHAPTER 6

Searching for Brumby Cloverpatch

As much as she tried to blend in, Daring Do could not help standing out as she made her way through the town. It wasn't just that she was the only Pegasus in sight, but her style of dress was also completely different from the local ponies of Alto Terre. While Daring wore her usual green, collared adventure shirt and matching pith helmet, they wore decorated sashes, furry boots over their hooves, and floppy caps. Truthfully, it was more impractical clothing than one might have imagined a society of mountain ponies to don.

It didn't matter, though, because Daring employed the use of disguises whenever she could. They seemed to make everypony feel more at ease with her presence, whatever the mission happened to be. She would put a stop to the sideways glances and whispers she was stirring up with each step closer to the village square. As she scanned the area for signs of Brumby, Daring Do also kept an eye out for a shop in which she might purchase some Alto Terran attire.

"Excuse me, ladies." Daring Do held

a hoof up to a group of chatty ponies crossing in front of her. They stopped and looked at her quizzically, and Daring found herself doing the same back to them once she got a closer look at the company. These ponies—the residents of Alto Terre—all seemed to share another trait that she had never seen before. They were monochromatic! If a pony was yellow, so was her mane and tail, along with the clothes she wore. If a stallion was blue, so was the rest of him. They wore different shades of their given color, but chose to stick to the one they'd been born with. It was quite the change from the rainbow variations of the ponies back home and throughout most of Equestria, and Daring found it peculiar, to say the least.

A purple mare with a rich, plum-colored

sash stepped forward to break the stale-
mate. Her voice was squeaky and high-
pitched. "Did you need something?" she
asked, raising a brow quizzically.

"What?" replied Daring Do, snapping
out of her train of thought about monochromatic coat color and what it might
mean. "Oh yes! I was wondering if you
might be able to tell me where to find a
Mr. Brumby Cloverpatch?"

At the mention of his name, the mare
exchanged a strange look with her friends.
A light-orange mare standing next to her
looked Daring Do up and down and then
whispered something in her friend's ear.
A few of the others nodded in agreement.
The purple one turned back to Daring
and simply declared, *"No."*

The group trotted away, turning around every so often to gawk at the golden stranger with the multicolored gray mane, odd apparel, and set of wings. Daring shrugged off the encounter and continued on with her mission. Just because some snooty gang of mountain mares had snubbed her didn't mean that she was any less determined.

It had been a long shot that the first pony she'd ask would know where to find Brumby, anyway. The mares *had* behaved oddly, whispering to one another like that, but it could have been just a few innocent comments on the fact that Daring Do was an outsider in the town. The difficulty of the journey to reach Alto Terre must have made it a rare occurrence for a visitor to show up.

The winding cobbled lane to the right housed several businesses. A café, something called a "Hoofenshine," and a shop. The blue swinging sign poking out from a storefront caught Daring's eye immediately. MOUNT MONOCEROS ITEMS OF FANCY, it read in gold-leaf letters. Below the name, there was a drawing of a monocle and smaller letters that read FOR FANCY PONIES. Daring Do was pretty sure that she wasn't the definition of a "fancy pony," but took the opportunity to duck into the shop anyway. Perhaps somepony who was going to benefit from her patronage might be more forthcoming with information and point her way toward Cloverpatch.

A bell rang as she pushed the door open, carefully stepping inside, her dirty hooves loud on the creaky wood floor-ing. Craning her neck around, Daring Do gathered that she was alone. The shop pony must have popped out for lunch or perhaps fallen asleep somewhere out of boredom. It was the perfect opportunity to creep around and do some exploring without anypony watching. She wasn't sure why, but her heart began to pick up its pace.

The shop was stacked to the ceiling with colorful swathes of fabric draped this way and that. Hats of all sizes, along with a few other random items, filled in the gaps, causing the whole thing to look like it was about to topple over at the slightest touch. Up by the register, there was a chest filled with goggles like the ones Ravenhoof had given her, except these seemed like they were more of a fashion statement than a utility item.

But the main ware available was the regional Alto Terran sashes. They came in many different textiles and plenty of styles. Some had tiny bells stitched into the edges, just like the cape of Mooncurve the Cunning, and others were plain and unassuming. They came in velvet and burlap, and some even had pockets. A sign on the wall boasted that the store stocked SASHES FOR EVERY COAT COLOR. Daring noted that ponies made a conscious effort to match their clothes to the color of their hide, though the reason still escaped her.

"G'day, miss. Lookin' for something in particular?" The gruff voice startled her so much that Daring Do almost flew up to the ceiling. She spun around, expecting to see an ancient mare decked out in the shop's commodities, but instead found herself staring into the familiar face of Brumby Cloverpatch himself! Though the burgundy stallion looked a little softer around the edges, he still wore the same mischievous twinkle in his golden eyes and worn top hat on his head. She knew right away that it was him.

"Yes, actually," replied Daring Do, hardly believing her luck. She tried to play it cool. "I just found what I came for." She sauntered forward and grabbed a yellow sash to match her coat color. Daring smiled and threw it down on the counter with a flourish.

"Great," Brumby said flatly, then let out a hacking cough. "Just the sash, then?"

Daring Do leaned forward across the

counter. "No, I actually need one other thing as well...."

"We also have boots, goggles, and... carrots." He gestured to several large bushels of carrots in a basket nearby. "Take your pick, kid."

"The thing I need is *you*, Mr. Cloverpatch."

CHAPTER 7

An Adventure Pony's Agreement

The old pony leaped across the countertop and tackled Daring Do, summoning a brute strength that appearance did not grant him. "Who sent you here?" he barked in her face, breath hot with the stench of cider and pub fare. Then, in a whisper, he growled, "How do you know who I really am?" The stallion's eyes darted around the room and out the window, completely paranoid that a stray Alto Terran had witnessed the event.

But the shop was empty, and so was the lane outside. "I don't think anypony saw, Brumby," Daring said sarcastically as she pushed him away and pulled herself back up to her hooves. She gestured to the vacant street and laughed. "This is what you call a 'bustling city'? Dude, you have got to get out more...."

"Don't tell me how to live my life!" Brumby snarled. He trotted back to the counter. "Look, I don't know who are you are and what you want from me—but whatever it is, unless it's a sash and some boots, you're not getting it. Especially if it has to do with—"

"*Cirrostrata*," Daring interrupted, growing serious. "The Forbidden City of Clouds. You have to tell me how to find it."

"Get *out* of here." Brumby put a hoof to his eyes, mouth contorted in agony. He took off his top hat and put it on the counter. His mane was nothing but a few wisps of frizzy white hair. Nothing like the full mane in the picture she'd seen of him.

"No." Daring Do didn't budge. She stood as still as ponily possible and waited. There was no way she had traveled all this way to find Brumby Cloverpatch, just to be brutally rebuffed. "I'm not leaving until you tell me what happened up there."

Daring took a step forward. Cloverpatch appeared to be in intense pain. Maybe she should do something to help, but what? Another moment passed before he finally looked back up to Daring Do. His eyes had lost their twinkle and instead seemed dark and scary. "I said to git out, miss." He stood up and motioned to the door. "Before I call on my friends to have you removed from the premises. Alto Terrans don't take kindly to strange characters botherin' 'em, ya hear?"

The bell of the shop door jingled. A green mare trotted in with a smile. "Afternoon, Mr. Brown!" she chirped before perusing the new green sashes in the corner.

"G'day, Minty!" Brumby replied with a genuine smile. His entire demeanor had changed. Daring found the whole thing bizarre. But the fake name he was using, the threats he had made, and the complete denial of Brumby's former identity all served to fuel the fire of her curiosity even more.

"See you later, *Mr. Brown*," she quipped. "I'll send A. B. Ravenhoof your kind regards." Daring tipped her hat to the old stallion, gave him a wink, and trotted out the door. This was going to be more difficult than she'd anticipated, but Daring Do didn't give up that easily.

It was easier to blend in with the townsponies with her new yellow sash. And since Daring had also tied her gray mane up into a topknot, hiding it underneath her helmet, she appeared more monochromatic. After a few hours of wandering through the town observing the local customs, Daring Do found a comfortable room for the night at a charming pub and inn called the Ciderin' Stein. It was small, inviting, and had several resident cats roaming the halls.

Daring had just dropped off her belongings and sat down to order some supper in the pub when Brumby slid into the booth next to her. "Didn't catch your name earlier." He looked straight ahead, like he was talking to somepony else.

"Do," the adventurer replied, turning to face him. "*Daring* Do."

"Don't look at me, Do!" he hissed. "Do you want help or not?" Daring snapped her face back to look ahead, just as he was. Brumby coughed. "Sorry, kid. It's just that I can't be seen with you. Ponies around here *talk*." Daring chuckled at this, thinking of the few conversations she'd had with some of them and how they'd all given her one-word answers.

"Meet me on Mount Equuleus tomorrow at nine sharp, and I'll tell you about Cirrostrata." The old stallion took a sip of cider and cleared his throat. "Don't be late, or the deal's off."

"Got it," said Daring Do. She kept her voice even. Brumby didn't seem like he mirrored her excitement, and she was afraid of him changing his mind. "Thanks, Mr. Cloverpatch."

"Don't thank me. Only doin' it for Ravenhoof." Brumby downed the rest of his cider in one huge gulp. "And, kid— trust me when I say this. You're crazy for tryin' to go up there."

CHAPTER 8
Brumby's Secret Weapon

Daring Do tossed and turned all night, speculating about the secrets of Cirrostrata and what dangers she could be facing if she found it. She wasn't afraid. The excitement made the blood and adrenaline pump through her veins so intensely that she could think of nothing else until she reached her goal. The idea of the unknown was the most thrilling part of her job.

However, one thing was bothering her. Daring was still slightly worried that Cloverpatch would change his mind about helping her. The old stallion seemed just the type to do so—mercurial and grumpy. It was suspiciously fortuitous that he'd come around last night and found her at all, but Daring knew that Ravenhoof's name carried great weight for many ponies. She only used it when she had to.

At six in the morning, when the dawn was just beginning to break through the foggy glass, she finally fell asleep. It wasn't long until she was awoken by a young pony's voice shouting through the wooden door, "Miss Do! This is your wake-up call!"

"I'm up!" Daring Do hollered back, springing to life and checking her pocket watch in a panic. It was already eight. Thank goodness she had thought to arrange the call—she had just an hour to gather her things and get to Mount Equuleus. It wouldn't take her long to fly there. Her wings were in good shape, even if the rest of her felt exhausted.

The snow-tipped peak of Mount Equuleus came into sight, and Daring realized she hadn't asked Brumby where exactly they were supposed to meet. There were eleven minutes left on the clock until nine. But before she could start to fret, she caught a glimpse of a massive silvery balloon. The structure was inflating slowly, and Brumby stood next to it, pumping air with an ancient-looking contraption hooked to a big tank. It was the shape of an oblong egg, with a small fin and rudder at the back. A wooden gondola sat at the bottom, but it was still mostly covered by material.

"Is that…an airship?" Daring Do marveled as she found her footing on the ground.

"Sure is!" answered Brumby, a sense of pride evident in his voice. "Over a hundred years old, and she still works. Well, I think she does. I have to admit, it's been quite a long time since we took a ride." He pumped more air through the compressor, and it made a whistling sound.

"It's amazing…." Daring Do reached out a hoof to touch the silvery material. It glittered in the sunlight.

"She's called the *Reflector*. You'll see why soon enough."

Daring Do had read about airships in her *Encyclopedia Equestria*, but they were rare these days. The Aeronauts Society pin on Brumby's lapel in the old picture flashed into Daring's mind, and it now made sense how Cloverpatch had explored so many areas as an Earth pony. Over the years, Earth ponies and Unicorns had developed lots of ways to join the Pegasi in flight, and this was his. So this is how he'd gotten to Cirrostrata.

"Before I take you there, I need you to agree to do something for me." Brumby reached inside his tan trench coat and pulled out a white envelope. "All I ask is that if you make it into Cirrostrata, you deliver this letter."

"Seems easy enough." Daring took the letter from him with a shrug. "All right."

"If, for any reason, you do not get it to its intended recipient—you are to destroy the letter." Brumby grabbed Daring's shoulder and met her eyes. "Do *not* read it. Understand?" There was an odd desperation in his voice. She could hardly say no to the pony. After all, they needed each other.

"Of course, Brumby, old pal," Daring assured with a nod. His face broke into a slight smile. "Can you tell me about the treasure? The Halo?"

"I don't know much, but I can tell you what I do know. This isn't going to be easy—you know that, right?"

Daring smiled. "I like a challenge."

"Let's go, you insane Pegasus." He put

on a pair of brass weatherproof goggles and motioned for her to do the same. "I sure hope Ravenhoof wouldn't send me somepony who wasn't ready for this."

"I've never been more ready for anything," said Daring Do. And she meant it.

CHAPTER 9
Twenty-Two Revolutions

The two ponies had been gliding through the brisk air for several hours, but they hadn't actually traveled very far from Mount Equuleus. Daring could still see the recognizable peak in the distance. Next to it was the tip of Mount Monoceros. Alto Terre was fuzzy, but it was visible as well.

Brumby steered the airship in yet another version of the same ellipse and answered Daring's thoughts. "The reason that nopony can find Cirrostrata is that it's designed for them not to. All those years ago, I *accidentally* found it by doing this."

Daring raised an eyebrow in response. "By making giant circles with the balloon? We haven't gone anywhere, Cloverpatch."

"Precisely," Brumby replied. "See, on that day long ago, I was looking for a flat spot to land my balloon in the Unicorn Range." He rolled out a piece of parchment and drew a large circle with his quill. In the center, he marked the two familiar mountains and put an *X* on the spot where she'd met him that very morning. "I saw the spot on the side of Equuleus, and it looked all right, but not perfect."

The airship bore right as he steered it, concentrating very hard. Brumby continued, trotting back over to the scroll. "I decided to keep searching until I found something better." Cloverpatch drew several more ovals, each one slightly different from the last. "By the time I had given up on a better spot to land, I had made exactly twenty-two revolutions. I always like to track things like that...."

"So what does that mean?" Daring Do wasn't following the significance of the number.

"After the twenty-second circle above these very mountains, something strange happened." Cloverpatch began to pace the gondola in excitement.

"What was it?" Daring searched the drawing for some visual pattern that might reveal what in Equestria Brumby was getting at. All it looked like was a bunch of scribbles.

"I would tell you, Miss Do, but we're on circle number twenty-one right now and I think you'd better see it with your own eyes." He gestured to the front of the gondola. Daring held her breath as she watched, not knowing what she was even looking for.

Suddenly, the *Reflector* burst through a patch of clouds. Right in front of them was a beautiful sky park filled with grand statues, glittering rain fountains, and fluffy cumulonimbus trees. Everything was balanced on a sprawling, iridescent cloud that appeared to be almost a mile long.

"What…is this place?" Daring cooed,

drinking in the magical sight through her goggles.

Cloverpatch took off his top hat and laughed in triumph. "It worked!" He grabbed Daring and hugged her. "Truthfully, I wasn't sure if it would again."

"It's incredible! But why do the statues of the Pegasi look so strange?" The stone ponies all had long ears that hung down like those of a rabbit and three vertical lines under their left eye.

"This is the entrance to Cirrostrata, and *those*," said Brumby, pointing to the nearest statue, "are what the resident ponies look like."

"Let's go get a closer look!" Daring Do was practically jumping out of the gondola in anticipation. She had never seen anything like the park in her life! Were the statues made of clouds, too? They looked like real, solid marble—but that wasn't possible, was it? She'd been to tons of other aerial cities throughout Equestria, and all of the structures had been made of cloud. This marvel demanded closer inspection immediately. Daring raced to the door. "Can you hitch this thing some-where?!"

"Oh, 'fraid not," Brumby said wistfully, looking past the park and into the open sky. He threw his hat back atop his head and gave a little bow. "I'm leaving you here, Do. You're on your own now."

"What?!" Daring trotted up to her new companion. The news actually made her upset. Cloverpatch was rough around the edges and she usually liked to work alone, but knowing that he had once been a con-temporary of Ravenhoof had made her respect him.

"I can never return to Cirrostrata," Brumby lamented, turning toward the front windows. He let out a heavy sigh. "If the ponies caught me inside the city, there would be severe punishments. That's why I need you to take that letter to Dew Point. Remember, you can find her near the castle. Just ask around and I'm sure you'll—"

"Punishments?" Daring interrupted. She watched as Brumby riffled through a chest of wooden drawers built into the wall near the steering wheel. Finally, he procured a green grease crayon and a thin black band with some pieces of fabric hanging off of it.

"Just don't get noticed in Cirrostrata, and you'll be fine," Brumby warned. "They dislike outsiders even more than the Unicorns of Alto Terre." He trotted over to Daring and leaned in. "Keep these on at all times." He placed the black band with the fabric on her head. The two pieces of fabric were the exact same golden color as her coat and hung directly over her ears.

"Fake ears?" Daring laughed, lifting one up with her hoof. "This is ridiculous, Cloverpatch."

"No—it's necessary. Now hold still while I draw some lines under your eye." When Brumby was finished with her, he thought she could almost pass for a real Cirrostratan. Daring Do looked at her reflection in a small hoof mirror. She felt silly, but the way he kept insisting made her believe it was indeed essential.

"Well, I guess this is good-bye." Daring opened the door to the gondola. The fresh windy air flooded in. "Wish me luck."

"It's a little late for that," Cloverpatch replied with a laugh. "Your instincts are all you've got now, Do." He held his hoof to his hat in mock salute.

Daring Do saluted back and turned to the unknown, taking off into the cool air. When she turned back for one last look at the airship, she had quite a shock. The silver material reflected the sky perfectly, rendering the airship almost invisible. The name of the airship now made sense, just as Brumby said it would. It gave her hope for all the other tidbits of information he'd given her.

As she flew away, she thought she heard Brumby try to shout something at her, but there was no use turning back. The winds were too strong. It sounded like he was saying the word *chronicle*. Daring Do wasn't sure what he meant by that, but she vowed to keep a good record of everything that happened to her in Cirrostrata. That is, if she made it there at all.

CHAPTER 10

Whispers in the Wind

The sunlight was magnificent this high up in the clouds, streaming down onto the statues in shafts of brilliance, like natural spotlights. Tiny particles floated in the air in a choreographed dance of sparkles. For a moment, Daring Do wondered if she might actually be in another dimension.

It seemed outrageous, but it had happened once before in her search for the Eternal Flower. On the Isles of Scaly, Daring Do had gotten pulled under the water in the Grotto of the Moon. The pony had found herself in another place, one where she was able to keep watching the scene above her unfold while everything around her had been turned upside down. It could happen. So where exactly was she now, and how had this place appeared out of thin air?

The sky park was the only part of the city around. It was true that Ravenhoof and Brumby had both used the word *invisible* in describing Cirrostrata, but surely if she could see this cloud platform, the rest of it should be visible, too. There had to be answers somewhere around here, perhaps a secret gate or portal.

Daring looked around the pristine park. The shrubberies were all expertly maintained, fluffy and white, with spheres stacked neatly on top of one another like the Rings of Scorchero. Formidable statues of Cirrostratan ponies stood in straight rows between the cloud plants, each one five times the size of her. From the sculptures' uniforms, it seemed as if the ponies were mostly military heroes. They wore jackets with fringed epaulets on the shoulders and were decorated with varying stone insignia and badges. A statue of a beautiful mare in the distance was outfitted in a long gown and cape engraved with hundreds of tiny raindrops that were encrusted with real crystals. The thin silver band across her head suggested that she might be important, but Daring Do couldn't be sure until she read the name at the bottom. *"Duchessss Precipi-taaaa,"* the wind whispered in answer to her thoughts.

That was strange. Daring Do looked around in confusion, still hovering above the ground. Had the wind just *spoken* to her? There was nopony in sight. Daring's pulse began to quicken, and her senses heightened to alert. Daring put one hoof on her leather lasso, just in case somepony was lurking behind a statue, waiting to attack her.

As she moved quietly through the air, Daring scanned the faces of the statues, studying their sinister expressions. Her eyes fell on one that looked exactly like Dr. Caballeron. Had she seen it move? *No,* she told herself. *There's no way. . . .*

Daring Do hesitantly landed and took a few steps forward onto the soft, silvery grass. Was that her imagination, or was the cloud vibrating slightly with each step she took? As an experiment, Daring picked up her pace and brought her walk to a trot down one of the paths. With every hoofstep, the vibrating began to get more intense and the thunderous noise of crumbling stone echoed across the park. But everything appeared completely still. No avalanches in sight.

Daring trotted down the path and stopped in front of a statue of two Cirrostratan stallions. They could have been brothers. Their identical faces were sculpted into permanent expressions of intimidation, brows furrowed and jaws clenched. One had a cropped mane, and the other's was long and wavy. *"Sergeant Storm Bringer..."* the wind whistled. *"Major Morning Blade..."*

Daring spun around and shouted to the empty expanse, "Come out, Caballeron!" But nopony came out to greet her. "So you are going to be a coward, huh?" She listened carefully for more trick whispers in the wind, but it was difficult to hear anything over the loud thumping of her heart and the blood pumping in her ears. "I know you're there...."

Daring trotted farther down the path. With each step, there was that crumbling noise again! Daring hopped back and looked down to where her hooves had been. The ground was completely unchanged, no visible cracks. The wind began to whistle again, and a sense of foreboding washed over her. She wasn't supposed to be here, and her presence wouldn't go undetected for much longer. It might have already been too late.

Up ahead, Daring Do locked her sights on the statue of the duchess. Something about it seemed different from the others. It was benign. The luxurious folds of her exquisite gown and the pleasant expression on her face—the corners of the mouth turned up ever so slightly—were reassuring. And underneath the great stone beauty was an inscription, which might shed some light on what exactly Daring Do was supposed to do to enter the city of Cirrostrata.

CHAPTER 11

The Magic Monocle of Visibility

The inscription looked like gibberish. Of course it was in another language. The Cirrostratans were unique from other ponies in most ways, so Daring felt silly that she hadn't considered them speaking another language. Why hadn't Brumby mentioned this major detail?

She ran her hoof into the grooves of

the letters. Daring Do had never even seen symbols such as these, and she had scoured countless caves and temples over the years. These characters looped, bubbled, and flowed like the very clouds she was standing on.

"What does it mean—*Precipita*?" Daring repeated the name she'd heard, looking up to the beautiful duchess, trying to search her expression for clues. Facial expressions were universal, a dialect that everypony could understand, no matter who they were or where they lived. For example, Daring could tell that she was a good pony and a kind leader. Her expression said, "Trust me." But there was also a sadness in her that was harder to understand.

A gust of heavy wind whooshed down the path and lifted Daring up and away from her musings about the duchess. She tumbled along the ground, finally grabbing on to the base of an opalescent cloud shrub. Once it passed, she was able to pull her body up, noticing that she was face-to-face with the statue of an older, menacing count. The wind whistled, *"Count Cumulonimbussssss."* For the first time, Daring wasn't startled by the disembodied voice.

A glint of gold caught her eye. The statue of Count Cumulonimbus was wearing a monocle! It was the only piece of metal Daring Do had seen in the entire park. Everything else was made of stone, shiny white grass, or cloud marble—including the crown atop his head. It had to mean something. The way the light shone onto it practically begged for it to be pilfered.

Daring Do didn't need any more convincing. That monocle was already hers.

The adventurer sprang up and landed on the count's shoulder. A cloudy mist rolled across the park in great billows and waves, encircling the statues and shielding their faces.

"Intruder! Intruderrrrr!" something hissed as the magical mist swirled around Daring's mane and into her ears. *"Intruder!"*

Her eyes began to sting. She closed them tight and held them shut for just a moment. *Poison clouds? What was she going to do now?*

The goggles! They were the answer.

But just as Daring found them in her

satchel, her body lurched forward. The goggles slipped out of her hoof and fell down into the bottomless sky. Daring opened her eyes and whipped her head around to see the culprit who had shoved her. The mist had formed into a perfect likeness of Brumby. He threw his misty body against hers again, propelling her forward. Daring grunted as he knocked the wind out of her lungs. She blinked furiously.

"What do you want?" she cried out to the cloud Brumby. His face was grave, and he pointed his hoof toward the statue of the count. Cloud Brumby threw his body against her again, causing her to tumble right past the massive pair of military ponies—Sergeant Storm Bringer and Major Morning Blade—and straight to the hoof of the statue of Count Cumulonimbus. A glint of golden light pierced through the mist. It was the monocle that he was wearing.

"Take it..." Brumby's voice commanded as a gust of wind surged, causing his likeness to disperse.

Daring snapped to action, reaching across the count's face and pulling out the golden monocle. She was surprised at how little resistance it gave her. She looped the gold chain around her neck like a piece of heavy jewelry and jumped off the statue, narrowly missing a poison cloud headed straight for her.

Daring Do flew between the statues, darting up and down without a single look back. The edge of the park wasn't far—if only she could get away from the platform,

Daring could lose the poison mist. Daring dived down between the legs of a massive marble stallion.

"Intruder!" The alert seemed to be all around her. She heard it inside her mind as well as through her ears.

Daring pushed faster, beating her wings as hard as she could. She twisted her body, bearing right. The angle of the maneuver caused the monocle to swing up into her line of vision.

Suddenly, a vast metropolis of clouds extended before her into the distance. When the monocle fell away again, Daring couldn't see anything! It was remarkable. Cirrostrata really *had* been there all along but was completely invisible to her regular Pegasus eyes. She tore her goggles off in elation and affixed the monocle to her right eye. When she turned back to observe the destruction she'd caused in the sky park, everything looked normal— just as it had before she stepped hoof onto the platform.

Even from this far away, Daring Do could see that another golden monocle had miraculously regenerated on the face of the count's statue. As Daring Do flew toward her destiny, she couldn't help wondering how she would fare in a place where she couldn't trust her own eyes. For all she knew about Cirrostrata, Daring Do might as well be flying blind.

CHAPTER 12
The Invisible City

Cirrostrata was built from every kind of cloud known to ponykind and even some that Daring Do had never seen before. With its broad streets and narrow alleys, tall spires and low buildings, the outline of cloud against sky created an edge both jagged and smooth, like the edge of a sophisticated key. It was hard to believe that this massive city had been completely hidden from sight the entire time and that the town of Alto Terre lay just below, totally unaware of its existence. Daring Do imagined the monochromatic Unicorns, and Brumby sitting in his shop.

As she soared to the front gates, Daring noticed a thick golden band of light encircling the entire city. Was it a force field that allowed the city to remain hidden from sight? Or was it just for looks? Either way, there was no denying that there was something extraordinary happening here. It made the adventurer all the more eager to explore within its walls.

Daring landed on the soft, cushy ground and trotted toward the white iron gates. The metal swooped and swirled in intricate patterns, climbing up to an archway that bore a bunch of tiny circles connected to one another. Daring Do counted twenty-two—the same number of revolutions they'd made in Brumby's airship before the sky park had appeared.

There were no guards in sight, but Daring Do remained alert with each hoofstep she took. It was hard to trust one's eyes here, a place that was invisible a few moments earlier. Who knew what sort of cloaking spell the military might have? After looking to the left and right, Daring adjusted her pith helmet and the monocle, then walked through the gates. She held her breath, expecting an alarm to go off, but nothing happened. She was safely inside Cirrostrata.

The wide avenue ahead was lined with stately buildings, lush pillow willows, sky lilies, and hundreds of ponies milling about. Delicious scents wafted from the windows of restaurants, and on every corner there were street musicians filling the air with sweet, haunting melodies. It all seemed fragile, as if a heavy breeze could blow it all away, yet here it was, sturdy and real. Daring marveled at the semitransparent buildings, made from a type of cloud so delicate that the milky shapes of ponies were visible from the outside.

Daring Do was grateful to be wearing Brumby's clever disguise. She seemed to be blending in perfectly with the Cirrostratans, who appeared exotic and mystical with their distinctive rabbitlike ears and three vertical stripes underneath one eye. Some of them wore ethereal gowns and capes made of gauzy fabric, some wore monocles of gold or silver, but most were dressed like regular Pegasi. Daring just hoped nopony would notice that her hide didn't seem to be slightly glowing the same way theirs did. The phenomenon was reminiscent of the ponies of the Crystal Empire, whose shimmering coats sparkled like the gems that their city was built from.

As Daring Do drank in the intoxicating sights and sounds, she tried to calculate her next move. This was still business, and she had an important goal—find the treasure. Daring Do had located Cirrostrata and made it past the statues, so there was a good chance she might be able to find the Halo as well. But there was still Brumby Cloverpatch's letter to deliver to a pony named Dew Point in exchange for his help. She hoped Dew Point was an ally and would be willing to give her a clue to where or *what* the Halo might be.

There was just one little problem— Daring had no idea where to look for the mare. She couldn't just go up to any stranger and ask them. Her foreign dialect would instantly give her away as an intruder. Judging by the whispers of the wind back in the sky park, that was the last thing she wanted to be in Cirrostrata. So she wandered aimlessly, pretending to act as the ponies around her did.

But her gait had been a little too

confident. Though she did not realize it, Daring Do had already caught the attention of three mysterious uniformed ponies. They all began to trail her separately, lurking in the shadows and ducking just out of her eye line. Their commanders had spoken of a possible intruder at the sky park. Could this golden pony be the one? She *looked* like a Pegasus of Cirrostrata....

A few minutes later, Daring was turning a corner when the scent of cinnamon and sugar hit her. She suddenly found herself standing at the edge of a vast park. The sprawling expanse had a rainbow pond at the center and hundreds of multicolored tents scattered throughout its rolling hills. A statue of the same mare from before, Duchess Precipita, stood on her hind legs, holding a stone cloud in her hooves. The object sprouted droplets of water that rained down onto the pond, creating little ripples that looked like tiny Sonic Rainbooms.

An old mare sat on an overturned cider bucket at the corner of the park. Her eyes were closed, three blue stripes beneath the left one, and a satisfied smile danced upon her mouth. Around her pastel rainbow mane she wore a golden scarf edged in silver disks. A diaphanous patchwork dress hung loose on her tiny pastel-yellow frame. Her cutie mark was a silver circle surrounded by purple stars. She winked at Daring and motioned to a steaming tray of doughy apple pastries, topped with glittering sugar. Daring's mouth watered in response.

"Only three bits for a fritter, dearie...." the mare enticed, waving her hoof around in a circular flourish. "Made with real *Appleloosan* apples, too!" Daring cocked her head to the side. So they *did* speak her language! Daring exhaled a sigh of relief. It was going to be much easier to play the part now.

"How can I be sure..." Daring replied coyly. She took a step toward the treat cart and raised her eyebrows in mock suspicion. "...that they *are* real Apploosan apples?"

"Just have a taste and you'll see." She nodded wisely and then winked. "Grandmare Clement speaks only words of truth. Best fritter in the whole sky."

Daring Do dug in her saddlebag and found her velvet pouch of bits. She tossed three toward the mare, who caught and inspected them carefully. Finally, she reached to her tray and removed two of the warm treats. "I think I'll have one with you. Walk with me. It's been such a long time since I've seen you, my dear...." The mare's eyes darted around behind Daring Do.

"I don't really have the time, Grandmare...." Daring said, testing the waters.

"You must make time," Clement replied. She stood up from her barrel and put a hoof on Daring's shoulder. "Come along, now. To my tent." She leaned in to Daring's ear and whispered, "Clement sees all. I know that you are not a pony of these skies."

Daring's heart dropped into her stomach. Why had she been so foolish as to gamble everything just for a delicious snack? It was a rookie mistake, and Daring cursed herself for it. But something in the old mare's eyes seemed trustworthy. And she would have shouted out if she wanted Daring to be caught. "Okay, Clement. I'll go with you. But I'd still like my fritter, please."

"Have both." Clement smiled and passed them over. "You think I'm not sick of them by now?"

CHAPTER 13

In Clement's Weather Tent

"Welcome to the Tent of Fate...." said Grandmare Clement as she pushed the silver drape aside to reveal a shadowy tent, lit only by the dancing flames of candlesticks and small, star-shaped holes in the sides that were illuminated by the daylight outside. A hundred scarves in every imaginable shade of blue hung from the ceiling.

Upon the ground lay a hundred pillows, stitched in the same swirling patterns as the gates. A low wooden table sat in the center, covered in velvety cloth and crystals. And in the center, a purple orb glowed with the light of a very special magic.

"Is that a Future Crystal?" Daring breathed. Her eyes widened in disbelief.

Grandmare Clement was taken aback. "You've seen one before?"

"Once when I was a filly, on a trip to Saddle Arabia with my uncle Ad." Daring Do hadn't thought she'd ever see one again. Future Crystals were the most rare of enchanted items and could not be controlled with Unicorn magic. They required a bloodline—in order for the orb to work, it had to be given to a mare by her mother. In fact, they were rumored to have all been destroyed except for the Crystal Sphere of Khumn.

"Then you know how it works?" Grandmare asked, taking her place behind the orb. The candlelight on her face made her wrinkles stand out even more.

"I think of what I want to know about the future, and then you read the Crystal," Daring answered. "Except the Crystal always delivers two truths and one lie, and there is no way of knowing which is which."

"Very good, dearie." Clement smirked, waving her hooves over the orb. "Do you know why I brought you here?"

"Was it my disguise?" Daring flushed red as she touched the soft fabric of the faux ear. "I knew it wasn't convincing...."

"No, it was because you had three Agents of the Crown on your tail...." She looked around and brought her voice to a whisper. *"They're the personal henchponies of Count Cumulonimbus!"* Her eyes sparkled with the intrigue of impending danger.

"I did?" Daring Do tensed up, eyes darting around the tent, expecting to see them now. Of course, they weren't there. "Am I safe here in Cirrostrata?"

"You will be," said Clement, eyes fraught with worry. "As long as you don't do what that Brumby fellow did...."

Daring leaned in. Of all the things she'd expected to learn from Grandmare, it wasn't this. "You know Brumby?"

"Everypony does." She nodded sagely. "He was the only outsider to have ever made it past the gates of Cirrostrata. That is, he *was* the only one until you did so today." The old mare got up and busied herself with lighting more candles around the tent. She kept peeking through the tiny stars to the park outside, presumably to see if the Agents of the Crown were still lurking nearby. "But we're going to keep that a secret, don't you worry."

"What did he do…?" Daring asked, her curiosity mounting. "What happened to Brumby Cloverpatch here?"

Clement stopped and turned around, a wistful look in her eyes. "What's the worst thing that can happen to a pony?"

"They get cursed for eternity by dark magic?" Daring guessed, thinking of a fate she would not enjoy.

"No, but close enough...." Clement replied, taking her seat in front of the glowing orb once again. "He fell in love." Daring shook her head in sadness. "With our count's daughter, the *duchess*."

Daring tried to picture Brumby as a younger stallion wearing his top hat and waistcoat, operating his airship with hearts in his eyes. So much time had passed since he'd written that letter to Ravenhoof. Duchess Precipita must be an old mare by now, and her father, Cumulonimbus, an ancient old pony as well. Suddenly, Daring Do became very aware of the letter in her bag. The urgent one that Cloverpatch needed her to deliver. He'd said it was for Dew Point, but it must have really been for the duchess. "Was it Duchess Precipita?" Daring asked in shock.

"How did you know her name, dearie?" Grandmare Clement gasped and put her hoof on her chest. "Surely you cannot decipher our inscriptions...."

"The wind said it...." Daring explained. As soon as the words escaped her mouth, she knew it sounded crazy. Still, that's what had happened. "The wind told me about all of them—Count Cumulonimbus, Sergeant Storm Bringer, Major Morning Blade...."

"It's you!" Clement shouted, standing and pacing back and forth as she recited an old rhyme. *"The wind will speak to the pony from the peak. She'll be devoid of fright through her circle of light.* You're the one. The Keeper of the Halo of Cirrostrata!"

"*I'm* the Keeper of the Halo?" Daring Do repeated in shock.

"Yes, you're the one who is going to protect us. The Keeper of the Halo—the pony who keeps the light safe, keeps our world invisible from all those that wish to destroy us." Clement stared at the Future Crystal in excitement and anticipation. "Now let's take a look at how you're going to do it, hmm?"

Daring Do took a seat on a jeweled cushion and braced herself for the worst.

CHAPTER 14

The Guarded Castle and the Stained Glass

The trek through the heart of the city toward Castle Cirrostrata was longer than it looked. It zigged and zagged through tons of busy streets and past unsavory characters lurking in dark alleyways. Daring had lost the three Agents of the Crown who had been following her earlier by hiding in Clement's tent. It was impractical to risk running through the streets and drawing extra attention, in case more were hiding nearby. So in turn, Daring Do was forced to take her time trotting through the city, which was agonizing. It was like somepony had clipped her wings and she could no longer fly.

On the bright side, the long journey gave Daring Do plenty of time to think about what Clement the clairvoyant had told her. First there was the tragic story of Brumby Cloverpatch falling in love with the duchess and being sent away from Cirrostrata, then the intriguing theory that Daring Do *herself* was the Keeper of the Halo, and lastly—the three predictions of the Future Crystal. The information swirled around in Daring's head like the shining particles in the orb that had sealed her tragic fate.

Dew Point will betray somepony. One will be imprisoned. You will protect the Halo. Daring Do studied the words on a small scrap of papyrus. She hadn't wanted to forget the exact wording of Clement's predictions, so she'd hastily scribbled down the two truths and a lie. If it wasn't for the bad news, Daring might have treasured this paper more than some relics. To receive a reading from a Future Crystal was not an everyday occurrence. However, *not* knowing which of the three predictions was untrue was making her wary and unsentimental.

Any way Daring Do looked at it, something bad was going to happen to her.

Daring Do hoped that the second prediction was the lie. It didn't really matter if Dew Point would betray her, so long as she still ended up with the Halo and not imprisoned. That is, if there even *was* a Halo to find. The uncertainty of chasing after a magical item that might not exist only added to its allure. Daring pictured it in her mind, a golden disk filled with light, and tried to will it into existence.

Dew Point was the key, since she was not only Daring's point of contact for the letter, but she was also the best friend and confidant of Duchess Precipita. Grand-mare had never seen Dew Point herself but speculated that the noble pony spent most of her days around the castle at the top of the hill, trailing the duchess and attending to her needs. She was famous for her beautiful mane of silver and coat of gray. Her cutie mark was a blue rain cloud with three dewdrops, echoing the three stripes under her eye.

It was rumored that Dew Point was the only pony who could make the duchess smile ever since Brumby Cloverpatch had disappeared. It made sense that Brumby would want his letter to go to her. She sounded like a trustworthy secret keeper.

Daring Do stopped for a moment, and a group of gypsy ponies dressed like Grandmare Clement trotted past, mumbling to one another and pointing at her. "There's something strange about that golden pony's ears...." they whispered. "Is she okay?"

"I'm fine! Just a case of—" Daring trailed off, picking up the pace again until she stopped herself when the entrance to Castle Cirrostrata came into full view. The milky marble castle shone like the griffon's goblet. The tall columns and prismatic flags beckoned to her—a shining gem, floating above and spreading its light across the entire city of Cirrostrata. Daring shielded her eyes from the near-blinding beauty of the giant, carved opal in the sky.

The group of ponies had lost interest in Daring's strange ears and moved on; otherwise she might have asked them what the protocol was for entering the castle. There was a line of uniformed guards on each side of the wide steps leading up to the main doors. They remained still, faces so stern that Daring thought for a moment that they might be more of the enchanted statues.

She put her hoof on the lowest step, and the nearest cadet trotted over. "State your business, citizen."

"I'm here as a guest of Dew Point." Daring met the eyes of the military pony and announced this with a deep bow. "It's urgent that I see her."

"The Mare's Maid?" the statuesque stallion replied, raising a confused eyebrow. "Is she expecting you, miss?"

"Yes," Daring Do insisted, narrowing her eyes. "Please take me to her straightaway."

"Excuse me for a moment." The pony gave a cordial bow back and trotted over to his colleague, a scrawny stallion with an orange mane and a suspicious look in his eyes. The two whispered back and forth for a few moments, intermittently glancing over at Daring Do before trotting back over together. They cleared their throats and stood at attention before addressing her again. There was a protocol to everything, and it had been so long since they'd had a guest that they'd nearly forgotten how to act.

"Maid Dew Point does not usually have guests," Orange Mane said haughtily, looking down at her through his own thick glass monocle. He kept adjusting his white uniform. Every time he touched it, the shiny fringe on each epaulet rippled. "We shall escort you to her, but"—he squinted his eyes at Daring—"be forewarned: if you are lying about your appointment with the duchess's maid, there will be severe consequences."

"I assure you, sirs. Everything will be just fine," Daring replied with a convincing smile. All she had to do was get the letter to Dew Point. Once the pony read it, she would see that Daring was a friend of Brumby's and would go along with her plan to find the Halo and keep it safe. At least, that's what she hoped.

The two soldiers motioned for her to follow them up the steps. The sound of their brass shoes on the cold marble made a loud clip-clop noise that only ceased when they stopped every few levels to whisper to each other and look over their shoulders at the adventurer. Every time they did so, Daring smiled and bowed, laying on the theatrics. They seemed to like this until the trio was only a few steps from the top and Daring leaned down for too deep of a bow, causing the monocle to fall right off her face!

Suddenly, everything around her vanished and Daring Do was floating in midair. It was difficult to process that Daring really was still standing on the cloudstone steps of Castle Cirrostrata. Her first instinct was to spread her golden wings and flap them as hard as she could to keep her body afloat. The feathered limbs sprang out involuntarily, and Daring Do heard the voice of Orange Mane shouting, "What's happened to her?!"

"Nothing!" Daring Do fumbled for the chain she'd clipped to her green shirt, found the monocle, and popped it back onto her eye. The surrounding city was there once more.

"Just a little wing spasm!" Daring's eyes darted around to the guards and she let out a nervous chuckle. To them, it had probably looked very odd—the Pegasus stopping midstep, gasping and grasping at the air. They still hadn't picked up that her monocle was a magic one allowing her to see them at all.

"Is there something wrong with your ear as well?" Orange Mane sneered, pointing his hoof at her head. "It looks like you've severed it!"

Daring's hoof shot to her headband and sure enough, one of her fake Cirrostratan ears was dangling off the band to which it was sewn. A quick adjustment to her pith helmet to hide the seam did the trick. The soldiers exchanged another suspicious look before turning back around and carrying on up the stairs.

At this rate, it wouldn't be long before this disguise was completely ruined. Daring had to hurry and find Dew Point. She needed help and protection.

The cavernous halls of the castle smelled like fresh dew and sugar. The walls were lined with tall, stained glass windows that artfully filtered the rays of light, bathing the opalescent tiles of the floor with hues of pink, purple, orange, and gold. The colors of the dawn and the sunset.

Images of weather elements were depicted everywhere, frozen still by jagged pieces of hoof-made glass. A thousand fluffy clouds and lightning bolts, punctuated by raindrops and mist. The largest window, above a blue throne at the head of the main room, was a star-shaped creation that bore a single gold, horseshoe-shaped item in the center. It had lines of ochre and tangerine extending from it to represent the shining quality of its ethereal material.

"The Halo…" Daring breathed to herself, eyes wide with awe and wonder. She felt her hooves pulling her to the window like a moth to a flame. It wasn't even the actual treasure itself, yet it was more beautiful than any treasure she'd ever seen.

CHAPTER 15
Do or Dew

The noble ponies of the castle watched with curiosity as the new visitor grew closer to the stained glass window, hypnotized by its splendor. Having looked at the window every day of their lives, many of them thought the golden Pegasus's behavior was peculiar. But seeing the glorious stained glass window through a stranger's eyes reminded them why the Halo had been chosen as the symbol of protection for the whole city in the first place. It was a gilded crown of power, horseshoe shaped for luck. The perfect background to frame the thrones of their beloved Count Cumulonimbus and his sweet, sad daughter, Duchess Precipita.

"I hear that you have business with me?" Dew Point appeared at Daring Do's side, helmed by three other mares. They all wore silk gowns edged in white fur, as if they themselves were the wispy clouds that painted themselves across the sky before a tropical cyclone.

Daring noticed Dew Point's silver mane and instantly understood why the ponies of Cirrostrata spoke of it. It was as shiny as a barrel of diamonds after a rainfall. There were thin shocks of yellow throughout that appeared as if they pulsed with a tiny electric current. Every so often, they would sparkle like little lightning bolts. Her almond-shaped eyes were the color of sunset, and she had long, dark eyelashes. The stripes under her eye were barely visible, as they were the same gray color of her coat.

"I haven't any idea who you are or what you want...." Dew Point continued, looking Daring Do up and down. "Should I trust you, stranger?"

"Yes, Maid Dew Point." Daring bowed to her, kneeling her forelegs to the tiled ground. Daring spotted the two guards watching them. They looked hopeful for the mare to make a grand display of the fact that Daring Do had lied her way into the castle corridors. She lowered her voice. "My name is Daring Do. I have come to deliver an important message to you from Sir Brumby Clover—"

"Silence!" Dew Point barked, a smokiness taking over her eyes. "I know you aren't a pony of Cirrostrata. But, lucky for you, I already told the guards that I knew you so you wouldn't get thrown in the dungeons, or *worse*." She glared at Daring Do and looked around the room at the dozens of other court ponies watching their exchange. "Let's find somewhere safe to talk, shall we?"

"Lead the way."

Though she seemed temperamental, it appeared that Dew Point was on her side and had just expressed that she didn't want Daring to be thrown in the dungeons. *"One will be imprisoned."* The words from the Future Crystal floated into her mind. Could that be the lie of the three? Daring Do exhaled a sigh of relief.

Dew Point waved her hoof, and her three sidekicks bowed their heads and trotted away. "This way," she said, nodding her head toward Daring. The two mares continued on down a hallway, away from the other nobles, presumably headed to Dew Point's chambers.

They wove through the maze of the castle, passing by several rooms of Cirrostratan armor and paintings along the way. Every time, Daring itched to go inside and explore, to uncover some of the secrets of the City of Clouds and the Halo. However, Dew Point was giving the impression that there was no time for detours.

She was on a mission.

"So, where is the duchess?" Daring finally asked, craning her neck to see inside an open, yet empty sitting room filled with luxurious furniture in shades of ice and slate. They were far into the castle and hadn't encountered another soul in ten minutes.

"She doesn't see anypony." Dew Point sneered, and a few streaks in her hair sizzled with a tiny electric pulse. "I am the only one who attends to her." There was an odd sense of pride in her voice when she delivered the second statement.

Daring scrunched up her nose. "Ever?"

"Ever."

"Doesn't she get lonely?" The image of Brumby sitting in his little shop in Alto Terre all alone came to mind. Not so different, really. "Does she miss Brumby?"

"Shhh!" Dew Point hissed, looking around. She grabbed Daring by the collar of her green shirt. "Never speak that name here!" Dew Point released Daring and gathered herself. "Just *wait.*"

CHAPTER 16
The Hushed Chamber

Dew Point leaned forward to crane her neck around the corner of the hall, her silver mane spilling down onto the floor like a rushing waterfall. After a few minutes, she procured a heavy, rusted key and thrust it into the base of an urn filled with white sky lilies that was sitting on a marble column. The urn swung aside to reveal a handle, which Dew Point pushed hard with her hoof. The wall seemed to crack open. An edge like a bolt of lightning shot up the wall and curved back down to the floor. The wall slid open, the sound of heavy stone scraping upon stone creating a commotion that echoed down the corridor.

She led Daring into the room and slammed the heavy door behind them. At first glance, there wasn't much inside compared to the other grand chambers they had passed on their way. A few, low benches upholstered with simple gray canvas sat in the center, and a rough, braided rug of white and yellow covered the floor. There were no windows and no artwork on the stone walls, except for a border along the top, carved right into it. The pony figures on the frieze were very small but appeared to be depictions of Cirro-stratans doing normal, everyday activities.

"I know it's nothing to look at, but this room is perfect." Dew Point relaxed and smiled. "The walls are thick enough so that nopony could possibly hear us, even if we yelled at the top of our lungs!" She trotted over to one of the benches and sat, patting her hoof on the cushion next to her as an invitation for Daring Do to do the same. "Sometimes I come here just to think because it's completely silent. Listen."

It was so quiet that Daring Do could hear her heart beating.

"Look, I can't waste any more time. I

have to keep moving," said Daring Do, meeting Dew Point's eyes. "It's from Brumby Cloverpatch. I'm not sure why he sent it to you instead of Duchess Precipita, but there you go." Daring pulled out the letter.

"We were all the best of friends. Him, Precipita, and me," Dew Point said despondently, holding the letter in her hooves but not opening it. "Once upon a time, at least."

"*Were* friends?" Daring prodded. "What happened?" Daring had only known about the relationship between Brumby and the duchess. She hadn't thought there might be more to the story. It was like chipping away at a block of Cirrostratan marble.

"He was never supposed to be here in the city of Cirrostrata," Dew Point lamented, her pretty eyes growing wet with tears. "As you know, Cumulonimbus, Precipita's father, forbids outsiders to enter our sky. It never mattered much to us because we never expected to meet any outsiders. We knew nothing of other lands. Nopony had ever made it here since Comet Tail."

"Starry-Eyed?" Daring clarified. So Brumby hadn't been the first after all.

"Yes, the great sorcerer and astronomer. He visited Cirrostrata centuries before I was born," Dew Point explained. "Some legends say that he created the Halo. Comet Tail the Starry-Eyed looked up into the night skies with his telescope, and instead of constellations, he saw a beautiful cloud city. Naturally, he had to visit Cirrostrata to see it up close. It was more extraordinary than anything he had seen below. He had to preserve its beauty, to keep it safe. He made the Halo."

"Where is it kept?" Daring felt a surge of adrenaline. She was about to find out the secrets of the Halo! It was within her reach.

Dew Point laughed. "The Halo can't be *touched*. It is the golden light that keeps Cirrostrata safe from view. What you're referring to, Daring Do, is the Half-Gilded Horseshoe."

Daring Do turned over the new information in her head, trying to make sense of it all. She wanted to ask Dew Point a million questions about the new relic that was just brought to light, but she still hadn't even finished her story or read Brumby's letter yet.

Daring waited patiently.

"Precipita and I had given up hope of

ever knowing what another pony city was like. Then, one day, kooky Brumby showed up in his odd-looking sky vehicle and swept everypony away, even the count! Though Cumulonimbus still didn't like the idea of outsiders." Dew Point paced back and forth as she spoke. "When he and Precipita quickly fell in love, her father forced Brumby to make a choice: either he could stay in Cirrostrata forever and become one of us, or he had to leave this place and never come back. In the end, he couldn't give up his life of adventure…"

"…and he chose to leave," Daring Do said, finishing her thought.

"It broke Precipita's heart," Dew Point said before tearing open the seal and unfolding the scroll. Her eyes quickly scanned the page, and her face flushed crimson. The streaks in her hair looked as if they were sizzling with the jolts of electricity, but her facial expression was unreadable. She could have been angry or embarrassed.

"What does it say?" Daring sprang to her hooves.

"Nothing good," Dew Point declared, rushing to the door. She took one moment to turn around and look Daring Do straight in the eye before pushing it open with an electric jolt and slamming it behind her. Daring couldn't hear the sound, but she knew: outside in the hallway, the clicking of a rusty lock echoed down the hallway.

Dew Point had betrayed her.

CHAPTER 17
Written in Stone

Right there on her scrap of paper, the words couldn't have been any clearer. *Dew Point will betray somepony. One will be imprisoned.* There was no denying it—Daring Do had definitely been betrayed and was now imprisoned inside the muffled room with no visible escape!

No windows or doors other than the

way in which she'd entered, and walls so thick that if one screamed at the top of her lungs, nopony would ever hear her. But Daring Do didn't panic. Instead, she began to see the entrapment as a new puzzle. When approached the right way, every obstacle was.

A quick experiment in removing the monocle from her eye determined that even if Daring Do *could* see the sky around her, she was still hopelessly trapped. And it was just too strange, seeing the ground below and not being able to reach it. She decided to put the monocle back on in favor of her own sanity.

Daring paced around, rubbing her chin with her hoof in a thoughtful manner. "Dew Point opened the door via a thin crack in the stone, so there must be another here somewhere," she muttered aloud. She began to inspect every inch and edge of the wall, searching for tiny seams in the stone slabs. When nothing turned up, Daring looked for patterns in the marble, starting from the ground.

When she reached the frieze near the ceiling, she noticed something extraordinary. The carvings that were too small to view from the floor were actually very intricate and beautiful. She saw depictions of the ruler and his guards, the legendary visit from Comet Tail the Starry-Eyed, and the birth of Duchess Precipita. It was the history of the Cirrostratans told through images.

Daring soon lost track of the minutes,

and then the hours. She was learning so much about the mysterious city and its inhabitants that she forgot she was imprisoned at all. The pony hovered near the ceiling, beating her wings to stay afloat as she smoothed her hoof over the expert carvings and leaned in close to inspect every last detail.

Near the end of the last panel of the fourth wall, Daring Do had a shock. There was a tiny version of herself staring back at her! The events of the day were all there: Daring stealing the monocle from the statue of Count Cumulonimbus, Daring walking through the streets of the city, Daring sitting inside Grandmare Clement's tent. The depiction was so detailed, she could even make out the tiny rip on her fake set of Cirrostratan ears. Then there she was walking along with Dew Point, finally sitting inside a tiny version of the very room she was in. The thought that there might be tinier carvings of the carvings made her head hurt.

"Fascinating!" Daring exclaimed, forgetting she was imprisoned. "The carvings magically appear as they happen!" As soon as the words escaped her mouth, Daring saw an image materialize on the wall. It was of the duchess galloping down a castle hallway, her cape flying out behind her and a look of concern upon her face. Surely she wasn't headed toward Daring?

Scccccccrrritch. The heavy stone skidded across the ground. There she was, Duchess Precipita, the heiress to the cloud city of Cirrostrata, standing in the open doorway. Her light blue coat was contrasted by her jewels—a thin gold crown and gold-latticed cuffs around her hooves. Her white mane was combed into a soft updo that accented her handsome cheekbones and big, bright eyes of yellow. "Brumby sent you?" she said, smiling at Daring. "I've been waiting." Her cheeks flushed pink. "For so long."

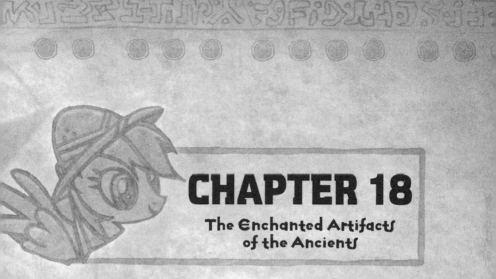

CHAPTER 18

The Enchanted Artifacts
of the Ancients

"This way! Quickly!" Precipita shouted to Daring, her eyes lit up with excitement. The two of them galloped through the corridors toward a secret escape door. Word had spread throughout the city that there was an intruder within the walls. Everypony was looking for Daring Do, who had a bounty on her head. Once the count got ahold of her, there would be no escaping. Precipita was desperate to help Daring Do, after she'd gone through so much to deliver the letter.

"Over there!" Precipita urged, pointing to yet another heavy door.

"Rrrrraw!" Daring growled, throwing her body against it. They tumbled out onto grass. The warmth of the shining sun and the chirping of the native birds were a stark contrast to the dark place they'd come from. Daring squinted her eyes, not realizing how long she'd been trapped inside the room of carvings.

They trotted toward a garden. "At first, I couldn't believe it when Dew Point said she'd left you there to keep you safe. But it makes perfect sense. Nopony ever goes in that room except me. Nopony else can even see the carvings."

"I saw them," Daring Do said nonchalantly, sitting down behind a tree. "And wait—Dew Point was trying to keep me safe? Not to betray me?"

Precipita sat, too. "Of course not! Dew Point can come off as a little bit mercurial, but she is my most loyal friend. And since you are a friend of Brumby's..." When she said his name, her voice went up an octave.

"He wrote to Dew Point because he knew it had a better chance of reaching me. When Brumby told me that he had never chosen to leave Cirrostrata *or* me but was forced into exile by my father, I knew it was time for a change." The duchess shielded her eyes and looked at the sky around them. "And the second part of the letter sealed my fate."

"What did it say?" Daring replied, scanning the sky. "And what are we looking for up there?"

"Brumby Cloverpatch's airship, of course! You didn't read the letter?" The duchess turned to Daring Do and took her hooves in her own. "All that time you had it?" She looked impressed and touched by the gesture. Maybe duchesses didn't get as much privacy as they liked.

"It wasn't mine to read," Daring Do replied with a shrug. "But if I'm being honest, I came here for another reason, too. I absolutely have to find the—"

"The Half-Gilded Horseshoe?" Precipita smiled and picked up the glimmering relic in her hooves. Daring couldn't believe her eyes! There it was, the relic that nopony was sure even existed. It was exquisite to look at, but knowing how powerful it was made it even better.

Daring couldn't take her eyes off it. "How did you know?"

"There is a lot I know that others do not. It is the curse and privilege of royalty." The duchess turned the shoe over in her hooves. Did she know how much this agonized Daring? "There is something that I need to tell you before I give you the relic."

"Go for it, Duchess." Daring's eyes traced the curve of the shoe and the thickness of the gold plating.

"Comet Tail the Starry-Eyed still lives.

He has gathered a secret group of prominent ponies across the ages to join him in his quest to protect the artifacts of our world. There's me—*Precipita the Caring*." She motioned to herself, blushing slightly at the title. "Then Rosewater the Cheerful, Mooncurve the Cunning, and Solar Ray the Candid." She paused for a second, considering her words. "And then there will be *you*—Daring Do the Constant. That is, if you pass the test."

"Me?" Daring pointed to herself, skeptical of being grouped with the famous sorcerers and important ponies. She was just a simple adventurer, touring the world and digging up old treasures.

"You are a protector of relics and preserver of cultures past! You were sent to me by them, I'm sure of it."

Daring wasn't so sure.

"It seems obvious to me now that the Magical Counsel of the Ancients should want you as a member someday. Your natural gifts of perseverance and courage could complete the circle of harmonized elements that are already joined together!"

"What if I don't want to join this secret society?" Daring Do replied. "I don't want to give up my life as an adventure pony. Nothing thrills me more than searching for long-lost relics."

"On the contrary, Daring! If you achieve this status, even greater treasures than you ever imagined will await you." The duchess smiled. "It is your destiny, so you would be wise not to fight it."

"But what if I fail?" Daring pleaded. "I don't even know what I have to do!"

"It is quite simple. You have already found many of the Enchanted Artifacts of the Ancients: the Sapphire Stone, the Rings of Scorchero, and the Eternal Flower, to name a few. Now you must continue your work and find the rest of the Sacred Twenty-Two, and touch each of them with your hoof." She made a sweeping motion with hers, and the glint of her golden bangles sparkled.

"I just have to touch them?" Daring raised an eyebrow. She thought of how she and her uncle had left the Eternal Flower back on the Isles of Scaly where they'd found it. And the relics of the Tricorner Villages, which needed to remain there to aid the ponies against the active Volcano. All she had to do was locate the items, to make sure that they were safe. "You can count me in for the challenge."

✦ ✦ ✦

When Duchess Precipita and Daring Do had finally made it to the sky park, where the royal assured her they'd be safe from the rest of the count's henchponies. *Cirrostratans are still too afraid to leave the city*, she'd explained back in the garden. *But soon, they won't be.*

"Daring, you must take the Half-Gilded Horseshoe, carry it somewhere far away from here, and keep it safe!" As she spoke the words, the duchess looked as if she were in pain. "It has already spent far too long in Cirrostrata, and it does many amazing things. It's a key as well."

"But—" Daring shook her head, confused. "I thought that the magic of the horseshoe was keeping the Halo activated here. If I take it away, won't your city be exposed to the world? Comet Tail linked their powers. Cirrostrata will become visible again!"

"That's true," Precipita said with a nod. "And it's scary. But I have a feeling that Comet Tail, wherever he is, would agree it's time to share Cirrostrata's beauty with everypony."

The wind was picking up. A heavy gust whooshed through their manes. Precipita's cape flapped dramatically in the wind. Daring Do wondered if the Halo was already weakened by the fact that the Horseshoe was getting father away. She took off her monocle, and in the distance, Daring saw the faint outline of a city coming into view.

"So you're leaving Cirrostrata?" Daring said as she held on to her helmet. "To travel the world in Brumby's airship?"

"A life without adventure can be a very dangerous thing," said the duchess with a hesitant smile.

"You know what?" Daring grinned, tucking the horseshoe into her bag where so many other treasures had rested safely before. "I couldn't agree more."

✦ ✦ ✦

And so, with the Halo dissolved and the Half-Gilded Horseshoe secured, the ponies of Cirrostrata were free to fly the skies once more. After Daring Do saluted the patient Precipita, who stood waiting for her first adventure, there was only one thing to do—take off into the open sky to look for the rest of the Enchanted Artifacts of the Ancients. Daring Do couldn't wait to see what she was going to dig up next.

THE END

A. K. Yearling's adventure novels starring the fearless Daring Do have been recognized as the bestselling series in Equestrian history. Yearling holds a degree in literature from Pranceton University. After college, she briefly worked as a researcher at the National Archives for Equestrian Artifacts and Ponthropology in Canterlot. During that time, she wrote an essay based on her findings of the griffon territories, entitled "What Was the Name of That Griffon Again? Or, Beak and Roaming Studies Recalled." It was published by the University of Equexeter's journal, *Pegasus*, last year. She enjoys quiet time alone at home and long trots on the beach.

G. M. Berrow loves to explore exotic locales around the globe, through both the stories she writes and her escapades in real life. Berrow is overjoyed to have collaborated on these adventures with her very own golden idol—A. K. Yearling herself! She adores shiny things, but she thinks the best treasure of all is a book.

GLOSSARY

A. B. Ravenhoof: Longtime mentor and friend of Daring Do. Before his retirement, Ravenhoof worked as an adventurer and a professor of archaeology at Pranceton University.

Alto Terre (OWL-toe TEAR-uh): An isolated mountain town in the Unicorn Range. The Unicorns in Alto Terre are unique because their coats and manes are monochromatic.

Brumby Cloverpatch: The Earth pony explorer who discovered the city of Cirrostrata in his airship. An old friend and contemporary of A. B. Ravenhoof, he now lives in Alto Terre and runs a shop.

Cirrostrata (sih-row-STRAH-ta): An invisible kingdom in the clouds, populated by a unique type of Pegasi with long rabbitlike ears and three vertical stripes under one eye. Cirrostrata has only ever been entered by one known outsider—Brumby Cloverpatch.

Comet Tail the Starry-Eyed: An ancient sorcerer and astronomer, he was the founding member of the Magical Counsel of the Ancients. Comet Tail was responsible for linking the power of the Half-Gilded Horseshoe to the Halo of Cirrostrata.

Count Cumulonimbus (kew-mew-low-nim-bus): The malevolent ruler of Cirrostrata. He despises outsiders and wants to keep them out of the cloud city at any cost. He is also the father of Duchess Precipita.

Curse of the Carthachs (CAR-haucks): A magical spell that causes ponies of other regions to dislike the high altitudes of the Unicorn Range. It was supposedly created by an ancient Unicorn clan called the

Carthachs in order to keep their rural home sparsely populated.

Dew Point: The best friend and confidant of Duchess Precipita.

Doomed Diadem of Xilati (ʃhee-LAH-tee): A sapphire-studded crown that belonged to the Empress of the Desert Skies. Its magic is tied to its sister, the Tiara of Teotlale.

Dr. Caballeron (Cab-uh-LAIR-on): A rival treasure-hunting pony. Ever since Daring Do refused to work with him as partners, he's made his bits by doing Ahuizotl's dirty work.

Ducheʃʃ Precipita (pree-ʃIP-ih-tah): The benevolent ruler of Cirrostrata and daughter of Count Cumulonimbus.

Future Crystal: The most rare of enchanted items. Cannot be controlled with Unicorn magic, and requires a bloodline—in order for the crystal to work, it has to be given to a mare by her mother.

Half-Gilded Horseshoe: A mysterious relic with many powers, including (but not limited to) keeping the Halo of Cirrostrata activated.

Halo of Cirrostrata: The invisible dome surrounding Cirrostrata.

Magical Counsel of the Ancients: A secret society of powerful ponies through the ages. Duchess Precipita believes that Daring Do might be a candidate to join their ranks if she can locate all twenty-two of the Enchanted Artifacts.

Monocle of Cumulonimbus: An eyeglass that allows the wearer to view the city of Cirrostrata. Daring Do finds it on the statue of Count Cumulonimbus in the sky park outside the city.

Tiara of Teotlale (tee-oat-LAH-lay): A crown that belonged to the Empress of the Desert Sands. Its magic is intertwined with that of its sister relic, the Doomed Diadem of Xilati.

Withers: One of Dr. Caballeron's henchponies.